Alvie
EATS SOUP

BY ROSS COLLINS

Arthur A. Levine   Scholastic Press

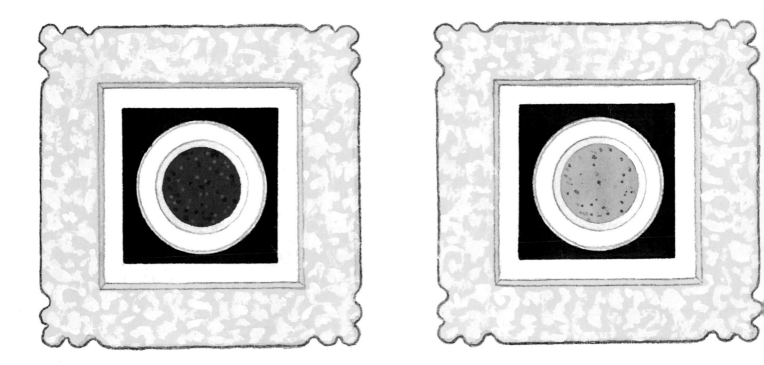

For Jacqui: hairy, crazy, lovely
— R. C.

This is the story of a boy called Alvie.

In the beginning
Alvie's first word was . . .

He's going to say Daddy!

said Alvie's dad.

He's going to say Mommy!

said Alvie's mom.

MULLIGATAWNY!

said Alvie.

Alvie had a little sister called Delilah.
Delilah could eat ANYTHING.

And at bedtime Alvie wouldn't listen to bedtime stories. Only recipes would send him off to sleep.

Mulligatawny Soup

1½ lbs lamb stew meat, diced
1 onion, minced
4 tbs butter
1 tbs curry powder
2 tbs flour
⅓ cup lentils
2 apples, diced
1 pepper, chopped
2 carrots, diced
1 tsp sugar
¼ tsp ground cloves
1 cup coconut milk

Brown meat in butter. Add onion, curry powder, & flour. Cook for 2 minutes. Add other ingredients except coconut milk. Add 2 quarts of water. Cover & simmer for 9 to 10 hours. Add coconut milk & serve with rice.

Granny Franny was kept in the dark.

15 Tureen Blvd.
Chowderville
G41 4NB.

RMAIL

Dear Granny Francesca,

Thank you very much for your delicious food
package. Alvie particularly loves the pecan
pie and the m

Alvie's parents worried.

They worried about growth.

They fretted
about nutrition.

They despaired over
what would be served
at his wedding.

But everything was pretty
much under control until one day . . .

They tried analyzing him.

Just as all traces of soup were hidden,
the doorbell rang.

Helloooo everybody!

said Granny Franny.

Once there Alvie's parents put their plan into action.

Alvie's mom ordered for everyone.

Everything please!

With so much food on the table,
Granny Franny couldn't possibly see
what Alvie would eat.